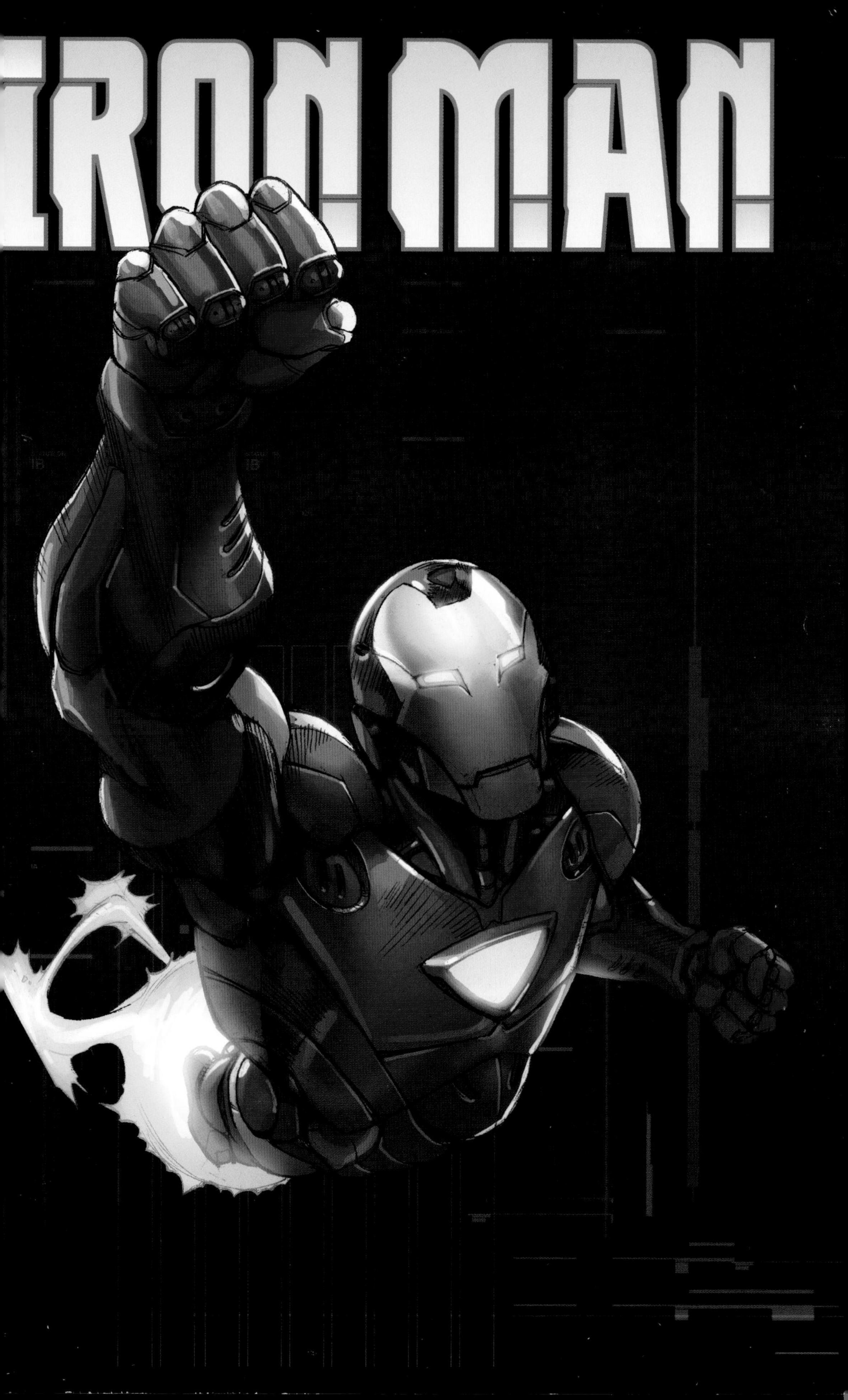
IRON MAN

**VISIT US AT**
**www.abdopublishing.com**

Reinforced library bound edition published in 2011 by Spotlight, a division of the ABDO Group, 8000 West 78th Street, Edina, Minnesota 55439. Spotlight produces high-quality reinforced library bound editions for schools and libraries. Published by agreement with Marvel Characters, Inc.

Printed in the United States of America, North Mankato, Minnesota.
042010
082013
This book contains at least 10% recycled material.

Library of Congress Cataloging-in-Publication Data

Van Lente, Fred.
 The bunker / story, Fred Van Lente ; art, Graham Nolan.
     p. cm. -- (Iron Man)
 "Marvel."
 ISBN 978-1-59961-771-8
 1. Graphic novels. [1. Graphic novels. 2. Superheroes--Fiction.] I. Nolan, Graham, ill. II. Title.
 PZ7.7.V26Bvk 2010
 741.5'973--dc22
                    2009052836

All Spotlight books have reinforced library bindings and
are manufactured in the United States of America.

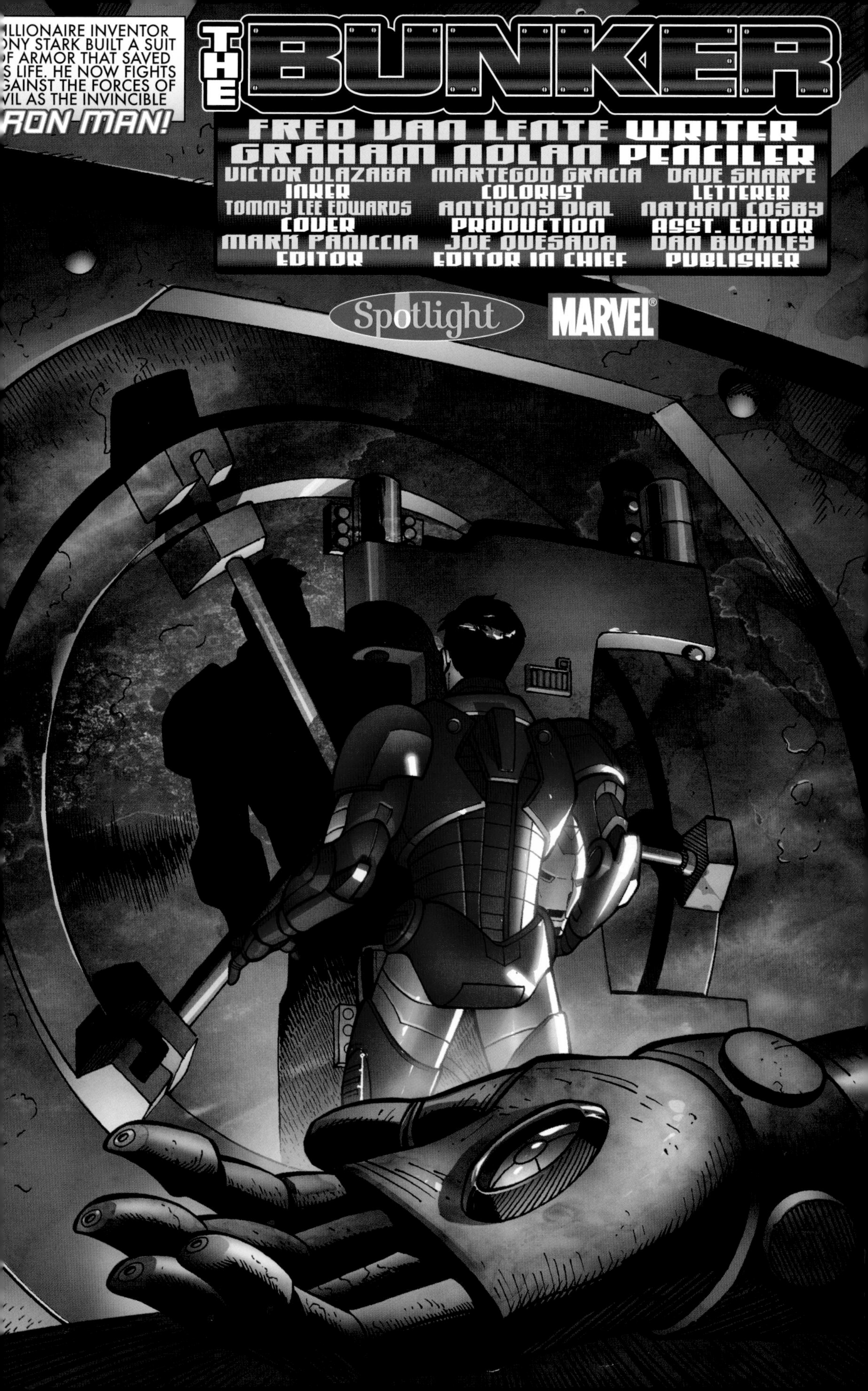
ILLIONAIRE INVENTOR
ONY STARK BUILT A SUIT
F ARMOR THAT SAVED
S LIFE. HE NOW FIGHTS
GAINST THE FORCES OF
VIL AS THE INVINCIBLE
RON MAN!
THE BUNKER
FRED VAN LENTE WRITER
GRAHAM NOLAN PENCILER
VICTOR OLAZABA INKER
MARTEGOD GRACIA COLORIST
DAVE SHARPE LETTERER
TOMMY LEE EDWARDS COVER
ANTHONY DIAL PRODUCTION
NATHAN COSBY ASST. EDITOR
MARK PANICCIA EDITOR
JOE QUESADA EDITOR IN CHIEF
DAN BUCKLEY PUBLISHER
Spotlight
MARVEL

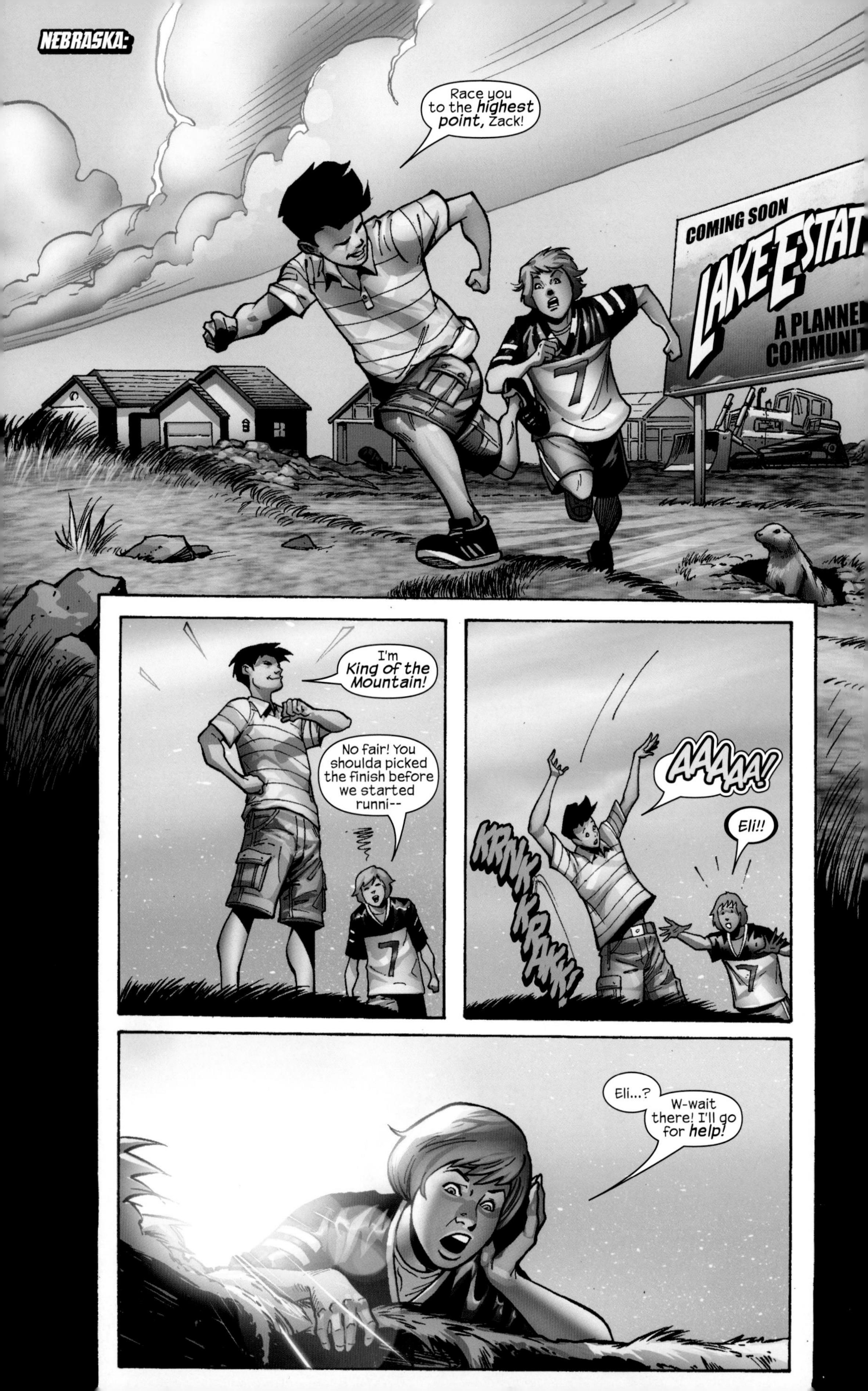
NEBRASKA:
Race you to the highest point, Zack!
COMING SOON
LAKE ESTAT
A PLANNE
COMMUNIT
I'm King of the Mountain!
No fair! You shoulda picked the finish before we started runni--
KRNK KRAKK
AAAAA!
Eli!!
Eli...?
W-wait there! I'll go for help!

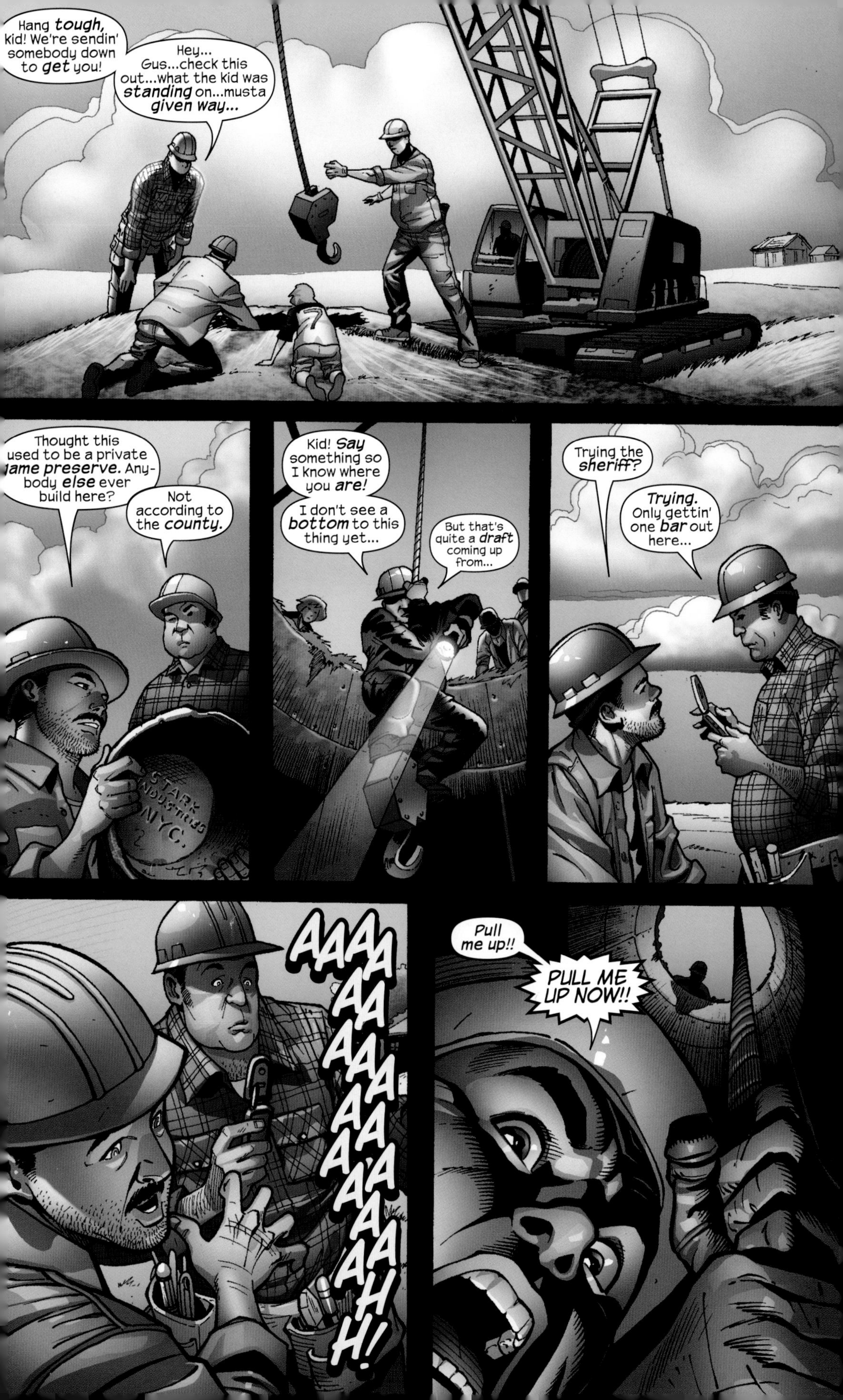

Hang tough, kid! We're sendin' somebody down to get you!
Hey... Gus...check this out...what the kid was standing on...musta given way...
Thought this used to be a private game preserve. Anybody else ever build here?
Not according to the county.
STARK INDUSTRIES NYC.
Kid! Say something so I know where you are!
I don't see a bottom to this thing yet...
But that's quite a draft coming up from...
Trying the sheriff?
Trying. Only gettin' one bar out here...
AAAAAAAAAAAAAAAAAAAAAAAAH!
Pull me up!!
PULL ME UP NOW!!

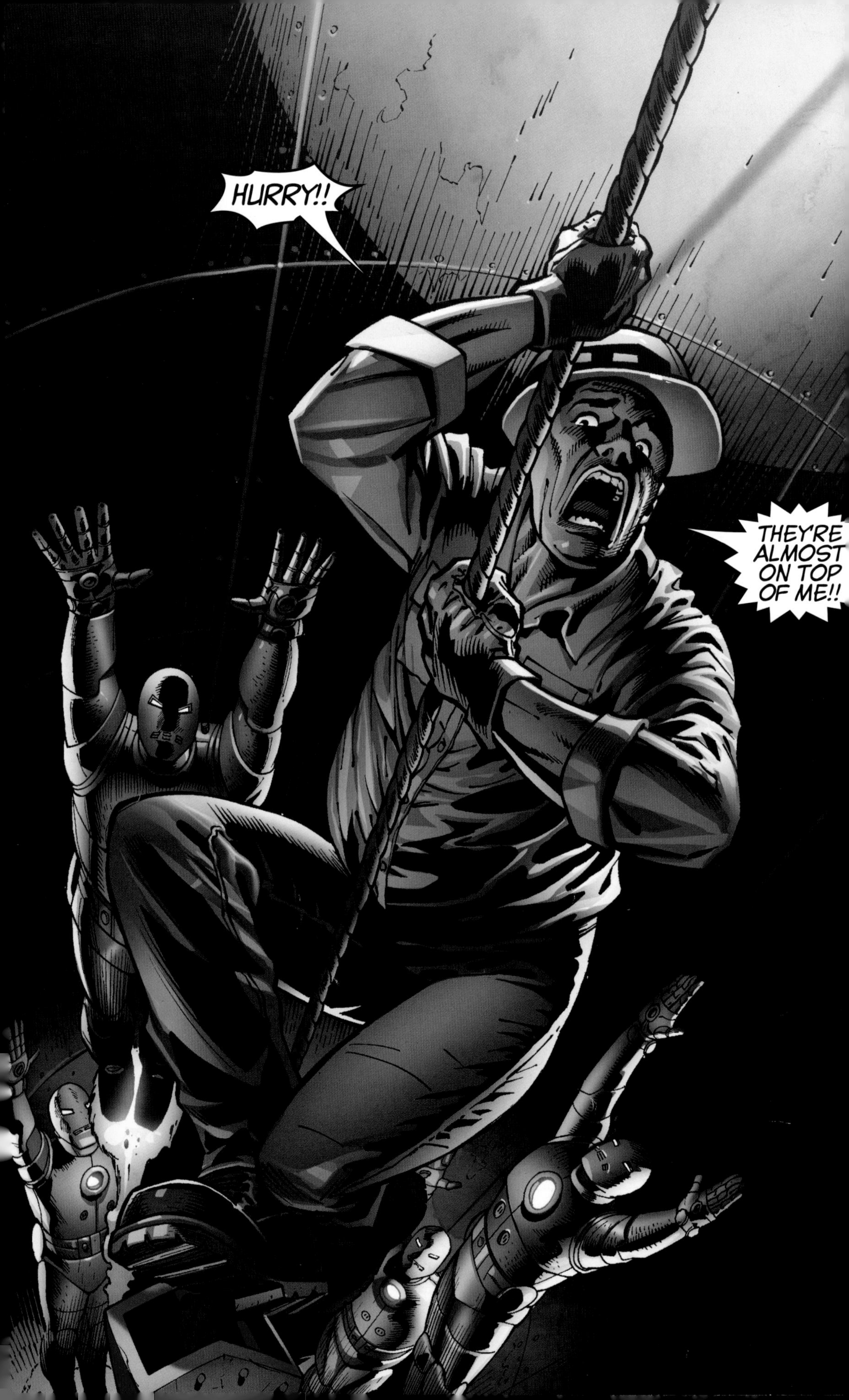
HURRY!!
THEY'RE ALMOST ON TOP OF ME!!

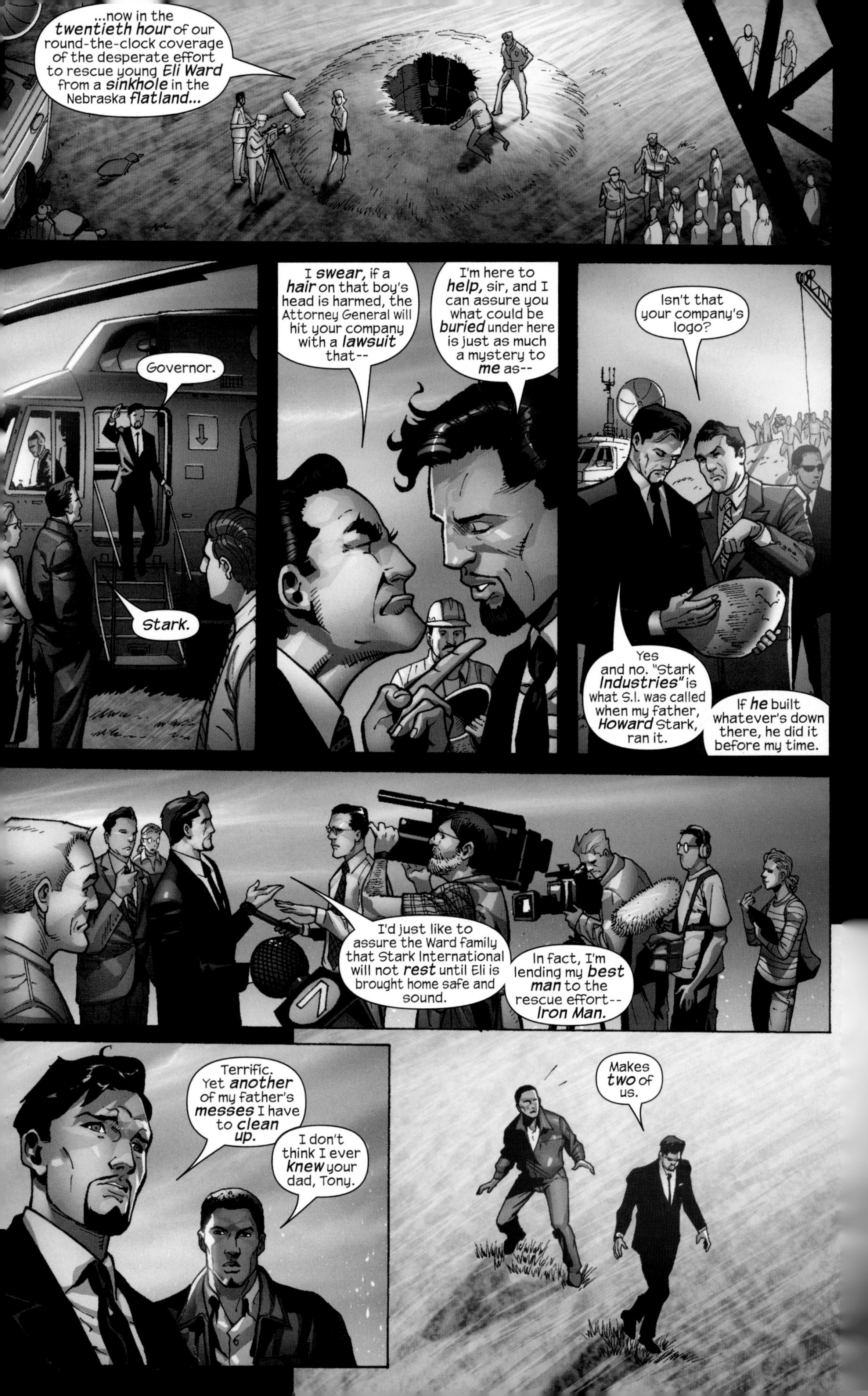
...now in the twentieth hour of our round-the-clock coverage of the desperate effort to rescue young Eli Ward from a sinkhole in the Nebraska flatland...
Governor.
Stark.
I swear, if a hair on that boy's head is harmed, the Attorney General will hit your company with a lawsuit that--
I'm here to help, sir, and I can assure you what could be buried under here is just as much a mystery to me as--
Isn't that your company's logo?
Yes and no. "Stark Industries" is what S.I. was called when my father, Howard Stark, ran it.
If he built whatever's down there, he did it before my time.
I'd just like to assure the Ward family that Stark International will not rest until Eli is brought home safe and sound.
In fact, I'm lending my best man to the rescue effort-- Iron Man.
Terrific. Yet another of my father's messes I have to clean up.
I don't think I ever knew your dad, Tony.
Makes two of us.

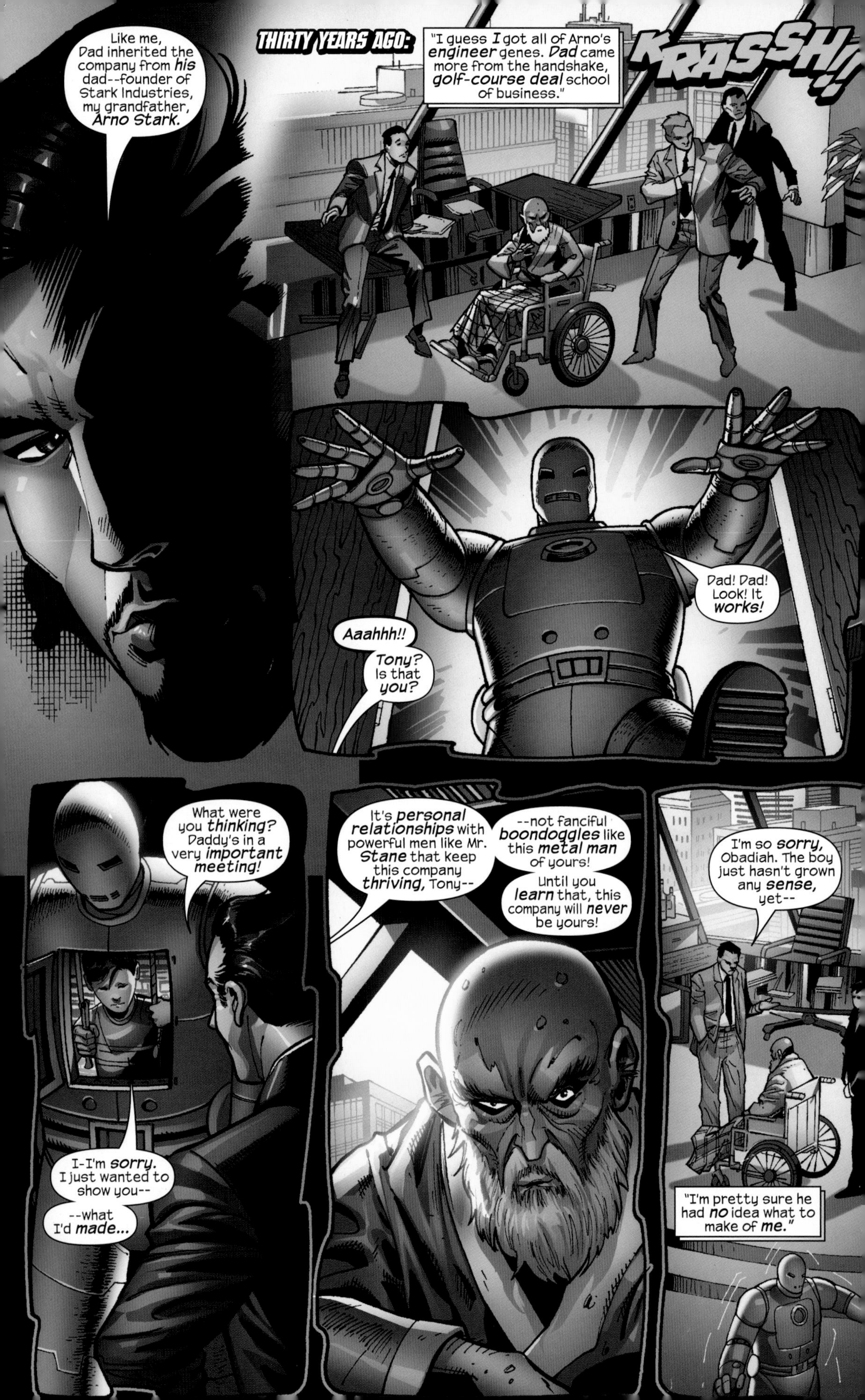
Like me, Dad inherited the company from his dad--founder of Stark Industries, my grandfather, Arno Stark.
THIRTY YEARS AGO:
"I guess I got all of Arno's engineer genes. Dad came more from the handshake, golf-course deal school of business."
KRASSH!!
Dad! Dad! Look! It works!
Aaahhh!!
Tony? Is that you?
What were you thinking? Daddy's in a very important meeting!
I-I'm sorry. I just wanted to show you--
--what I'd made...
It's personal relationships with powerful men like Mr. Stane that keep this company thriving, Tony--
--not fanciful boondoggles like this metal man of yours!
Until you learn that, this company will never be yours!
I'm so sorry, Obadiah. The boy just hasn't grown any sense, yet--
"I'm pretty sure he had no idea what to make of me."

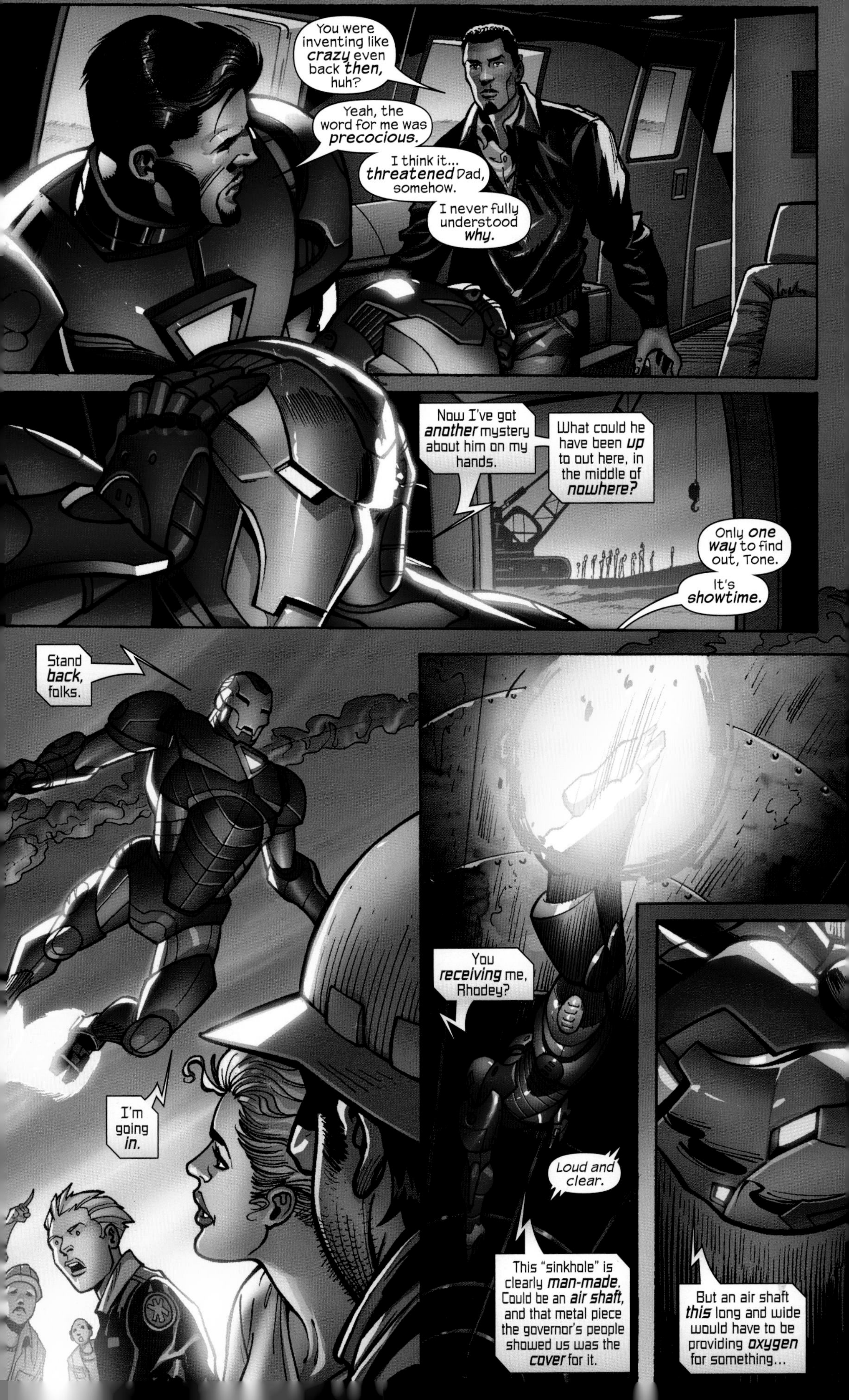

You were inventing like crazy even back then, huh?
Yeah, the word for me was precocious.
I think it... threatened Dad, somehow.
I never fully understood why.
Now I've got another mystery about him on my hands.
What could he have been up to out here, in the middle of nowhere?
Only one way to find out, Tone.
It's showtime.
Stand back, folks.
I'm going in.
You receiving me, Rhodey?
Loud and clear.
This "sinkhole" is clearly man-made. Could be an air shaft, and that metal piece the governor's people showed us was the cover for it.
But an air shaft this long and wide would have to be providing oxygen for something...

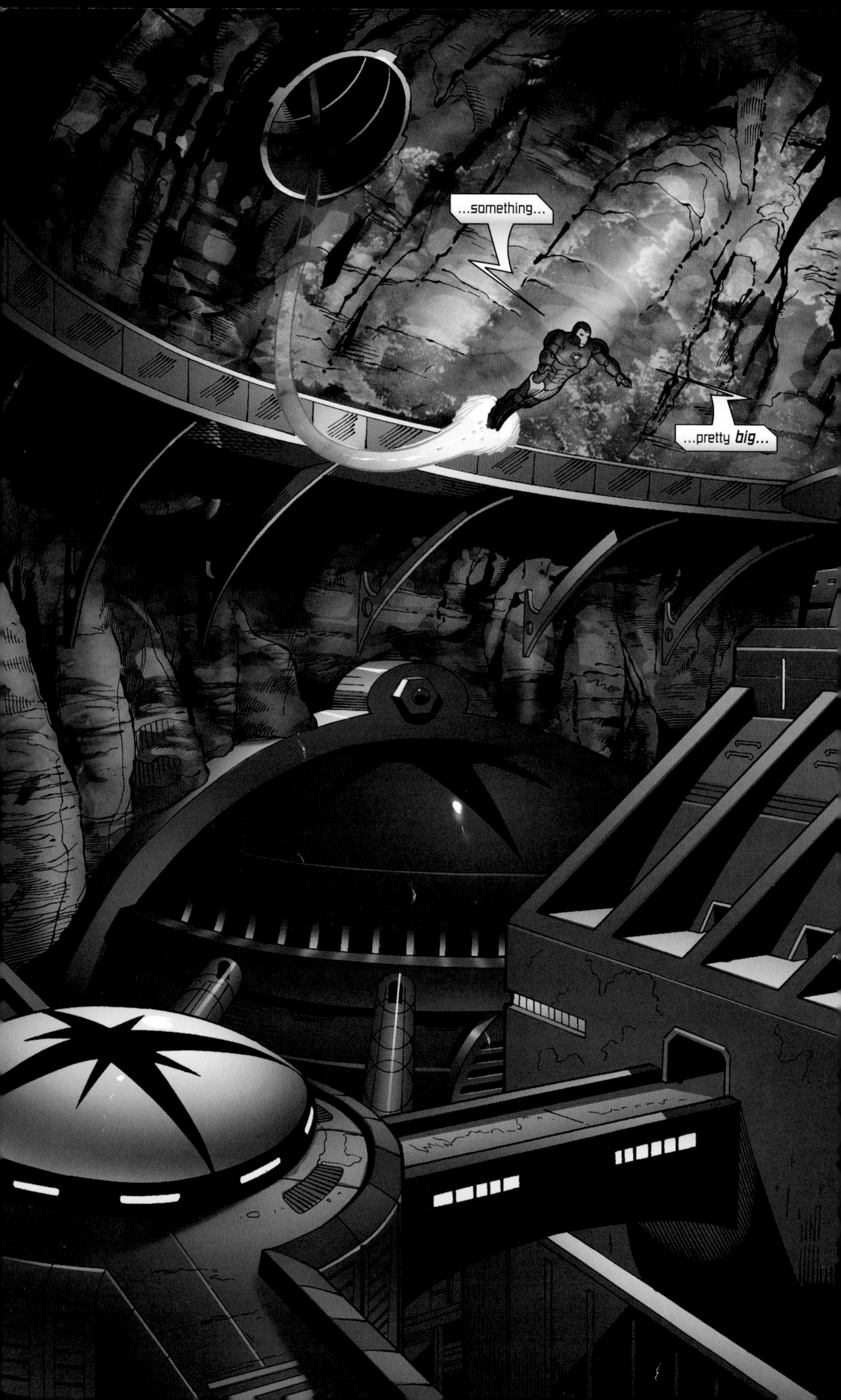
...something...
...pretty *big*...

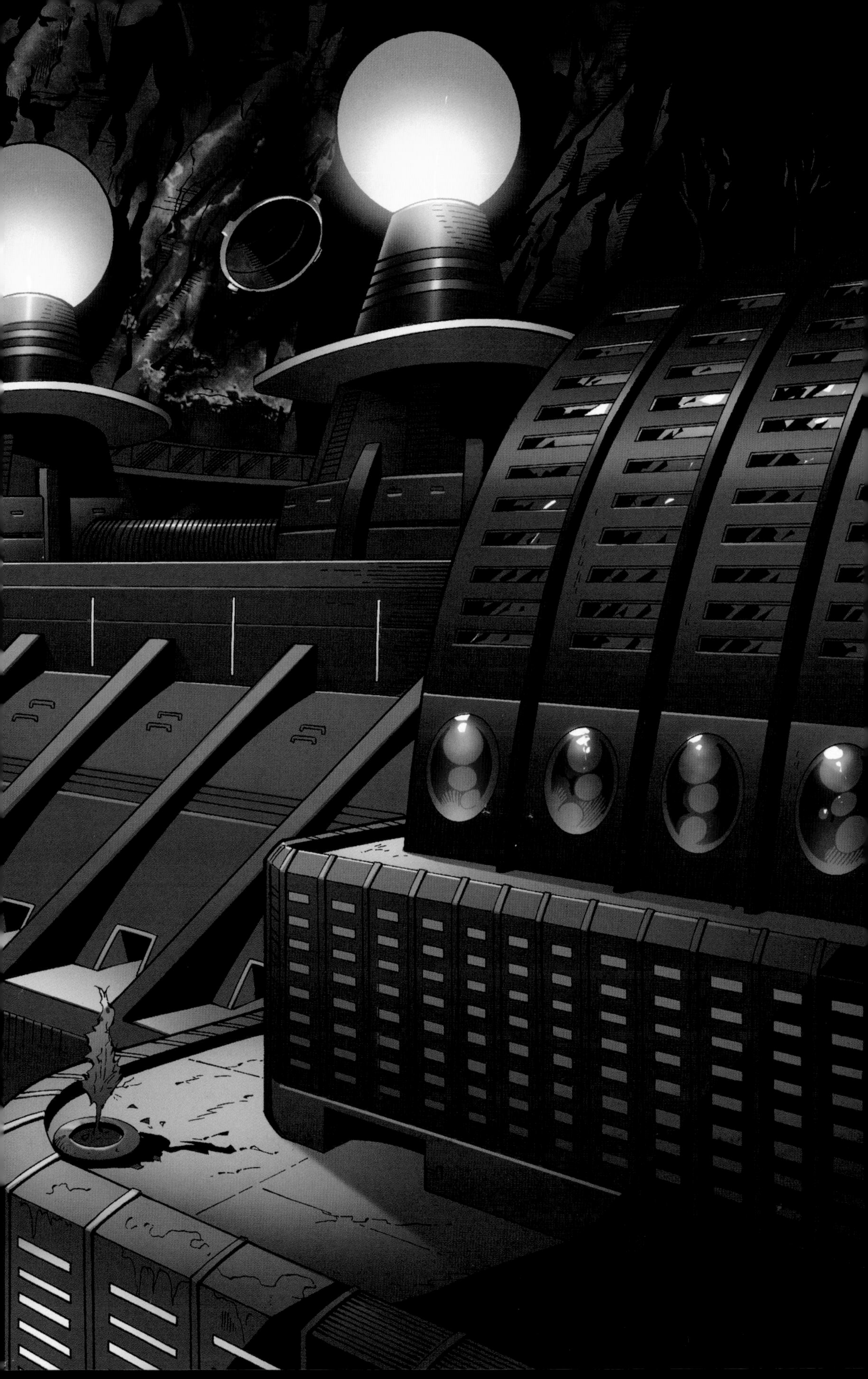

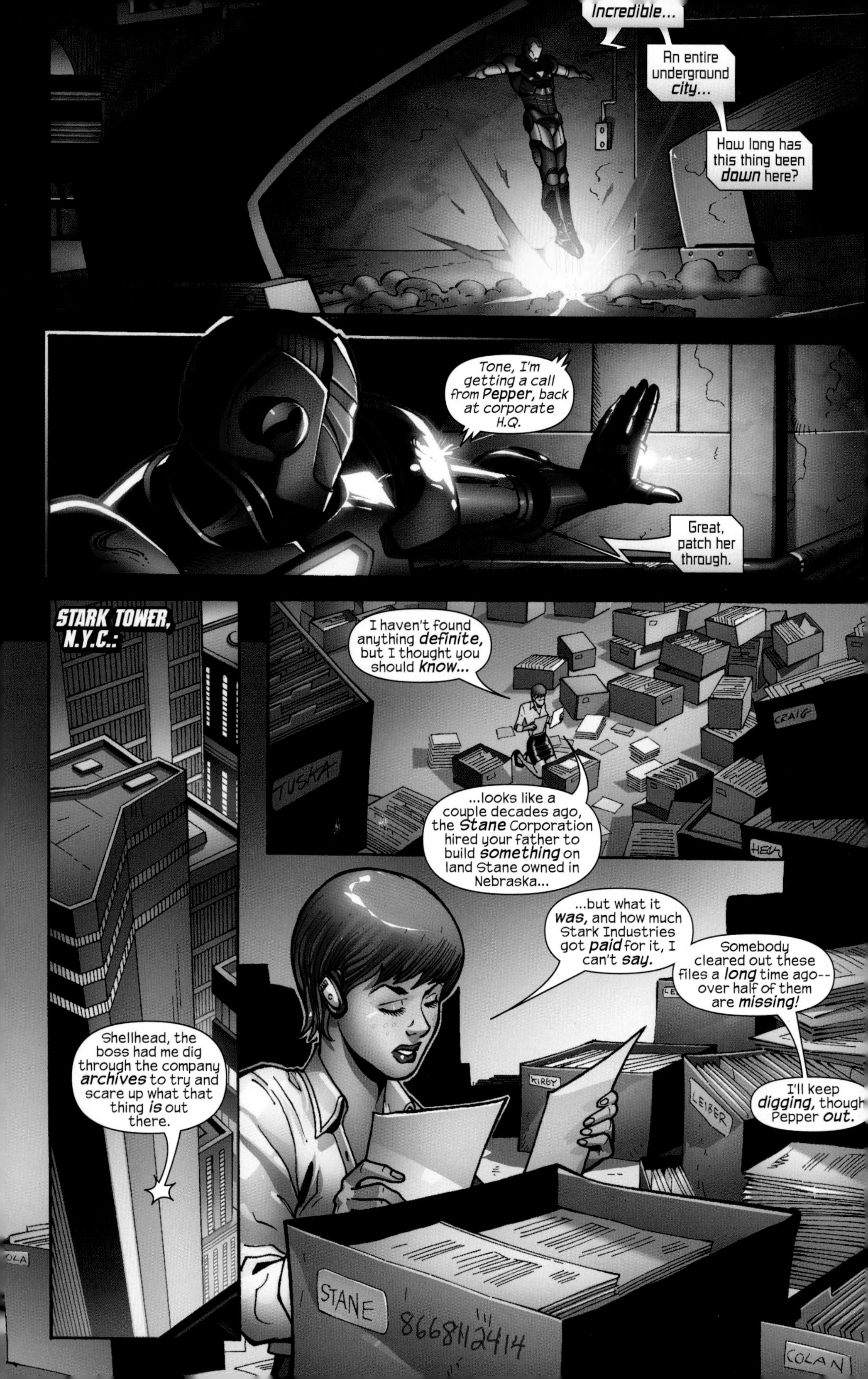

Incredible...
An entire underground city...
How long has this thing been down here?
Tone, I'm getting a call from Pepper, back at corporate H.Q.
Great, patch her through.
STARK TOWER, N.Y.C.:
I haven't found anything definite, but I thought you should know...
CRAIG
TUSKA
...looks like a couple decades ago, the Stane Corporation hired your father to build something on land Stane owned in Nebraska...
...but what it was, and how much Stark Industries got paid for it, I can't say.
Somebody cleared out these files a long time ago--over half of them are missing!
Shellhead, the boss had me dig through the company archives to try and scare up what that thing is out there.
KIRBY
LEIBER
I'll keep digging, though. Pepper out.
STANE
8668112414
COLAN

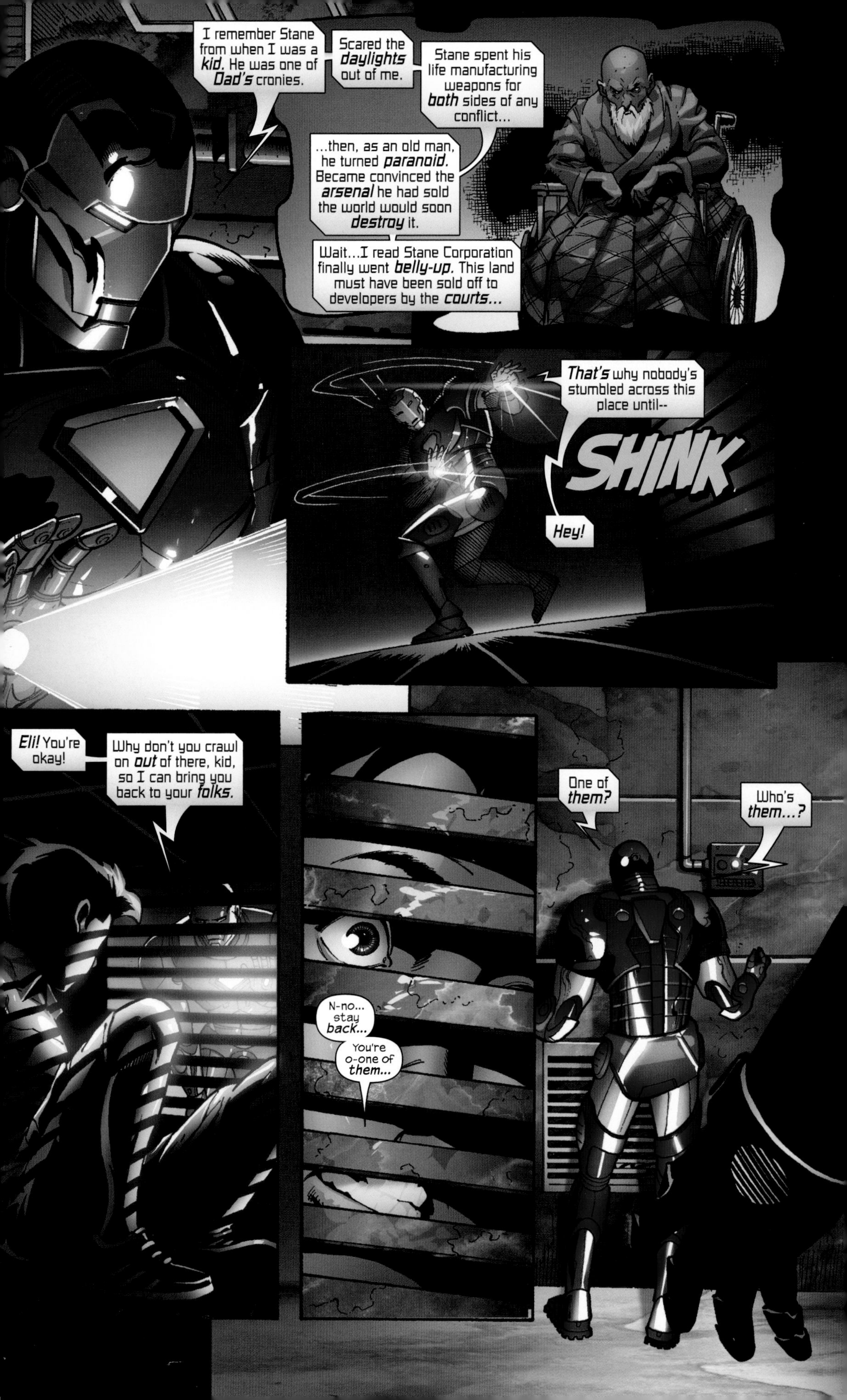
I remember Stane from when I was a kid. He was one of Dad's cronies.
Scared the daylights out of me.
Stane spent his life manufacturing weapons for both sides of any conflict...
...then, as an old man, he turned paranoid. Became convinced the arsenal he had sold the world would soon destroy it.
Wait...I read Stane Corporation finally went belly-up. This land must have been sold off to developers by the courts...
That's why nobody's stumbled across this place until--
SHINK
Hey!
Eli! You're okay!
Why don't you crawl on out of there, kid, so I can bring you back to your folks.
N-no... stay back...
You're o-one of them...
One of them?
Who's them...?

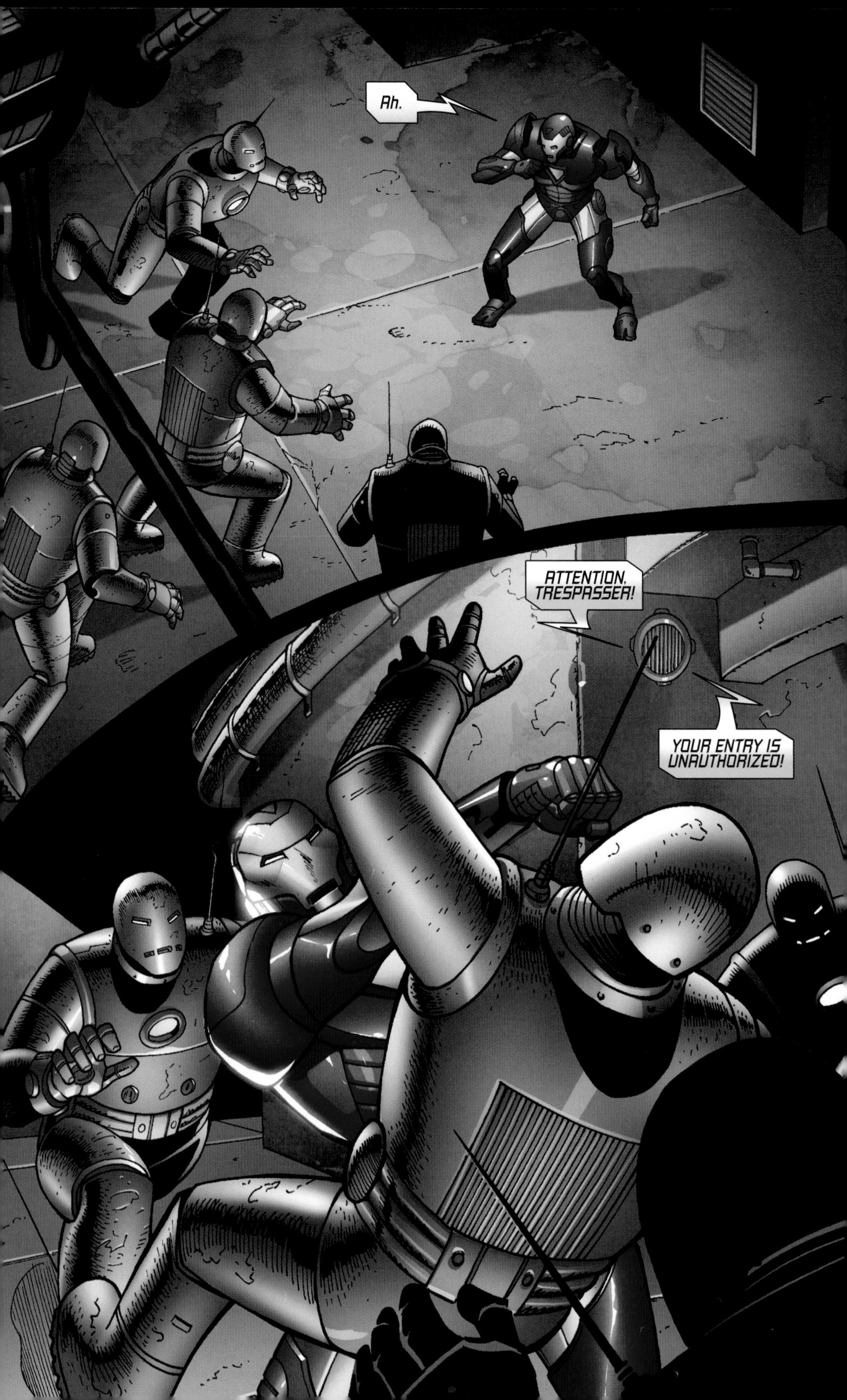
Ah.
ATTENTION, TRESPASSER!
YOUR ENTRY IS UNAUTHORIZED!

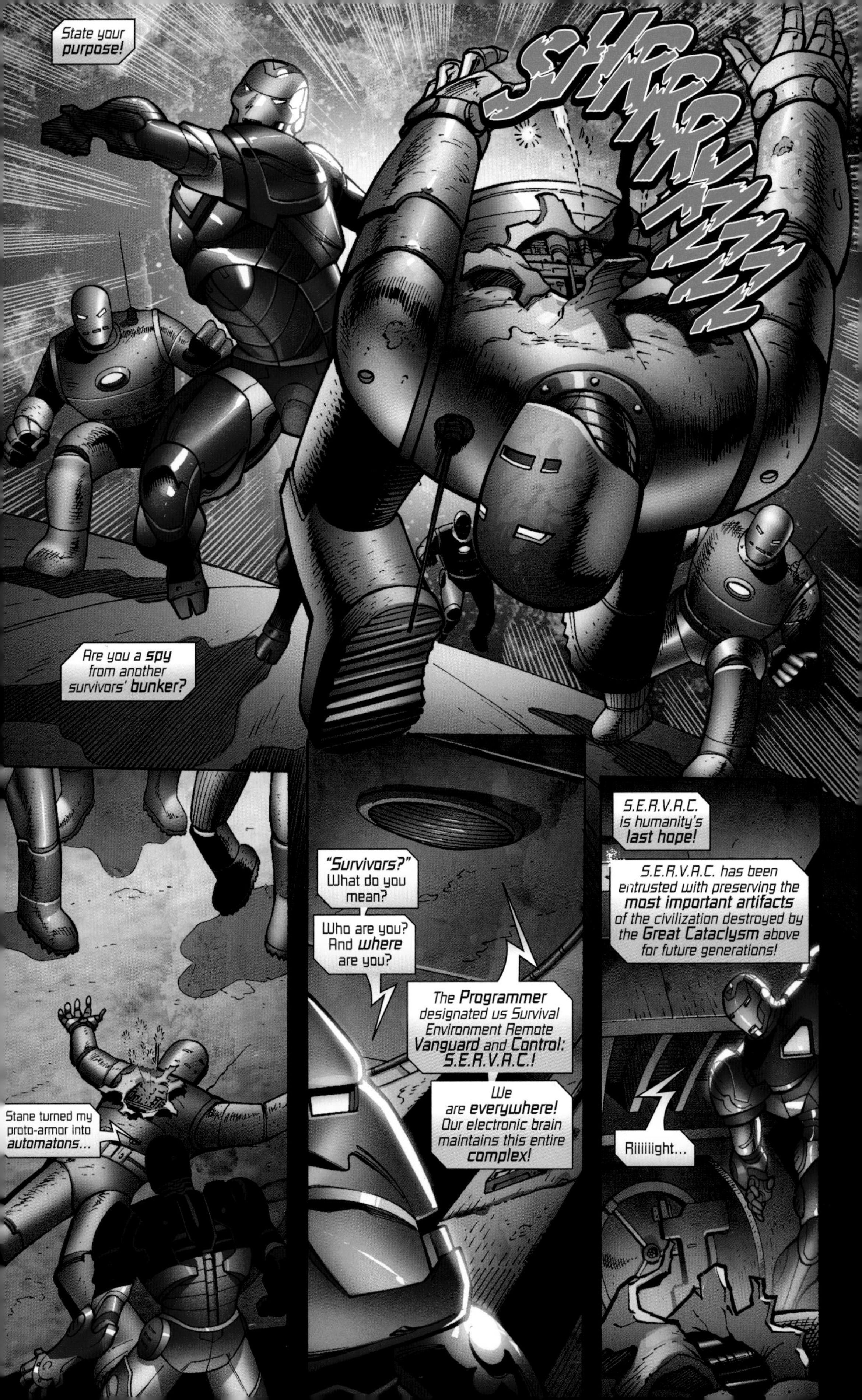

State your purpose!
SHRRZAZZZZ
Are you a spy from another survivors' bunker?
Stane turned my proto-armor into automatons...
"Survivors?" What do you mean?
Who are you? And where are you?
The Programmer designated us Survival Environment Remote Vanguard and Control: S.E.R.V.A.C.!
We are everywhere! Our electronic brain maintains this entire complex!
S.E.R.V.A.C. is humanity's last hope!
S.E.R.V.A.C. has been entrusted with preserving the most important artifacts of the civilization destroyed by the Great Cataclysm above for future generations!
Riiiiiight...

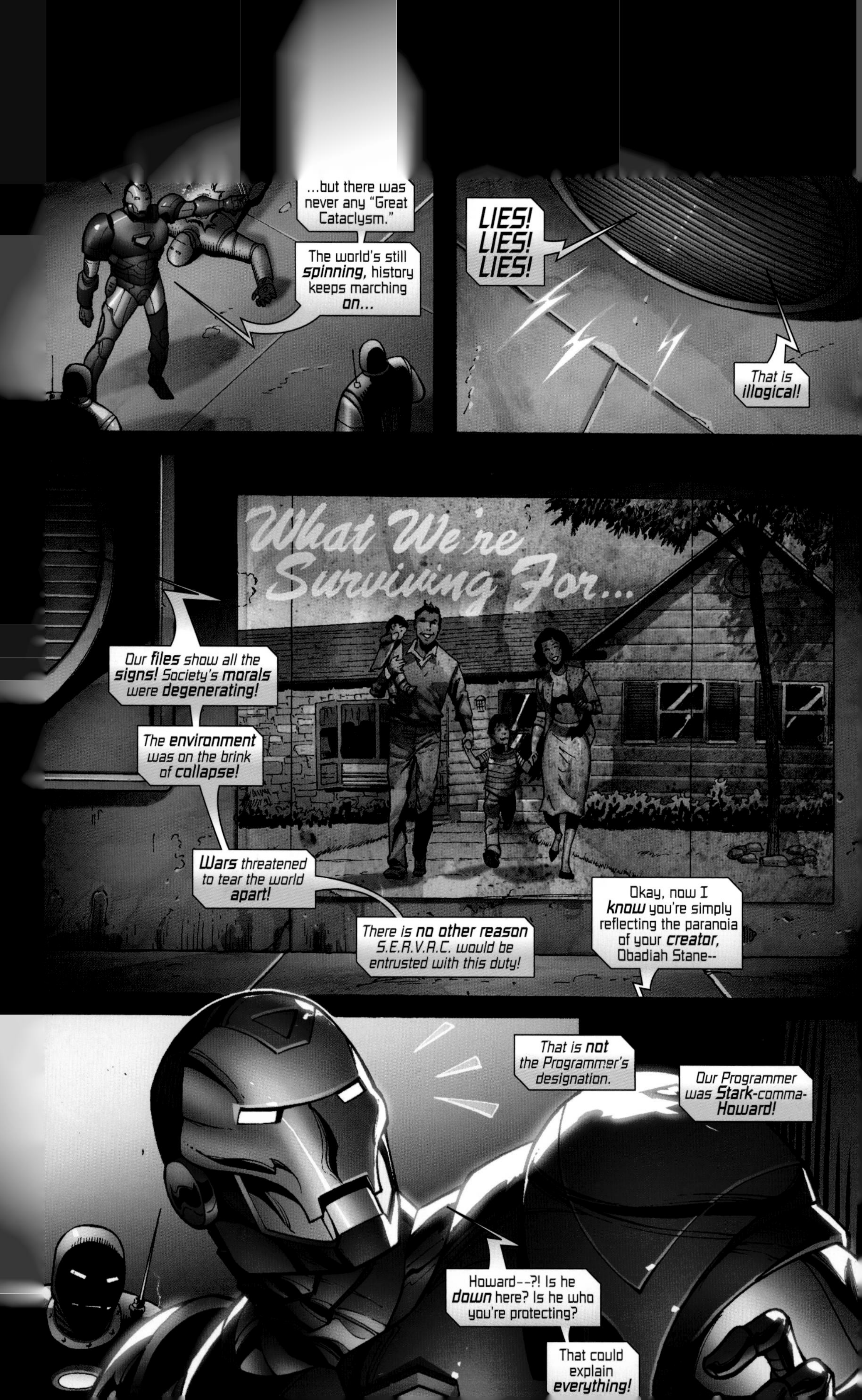
...but there was never any "Great Cataclysm."
The world's still *spinning*, history keeps marching *on*...
LIES! LIES! LIES!
That is *illogical!*
What We're Surviving For...
Our *files* show all the *signs!* Society's *morals* were *degenerating!*
The *environment* was on the brink of *collapse!*
*Wars* threatened to tear the world *apart!*
There is *no other reason* S.E.R.V.A.C. would be entrusted with this duty!
Okay, now I *know* you're simply reflecting the paranoia of your *creator*, Obadiah Stane--
That is *not* the Programmer's designation.
Our Programmer was *Stark*-comma-*Howard!*
Howard--?! Is he *down* here? Is he who you're protecting?
That could explain *everything!*

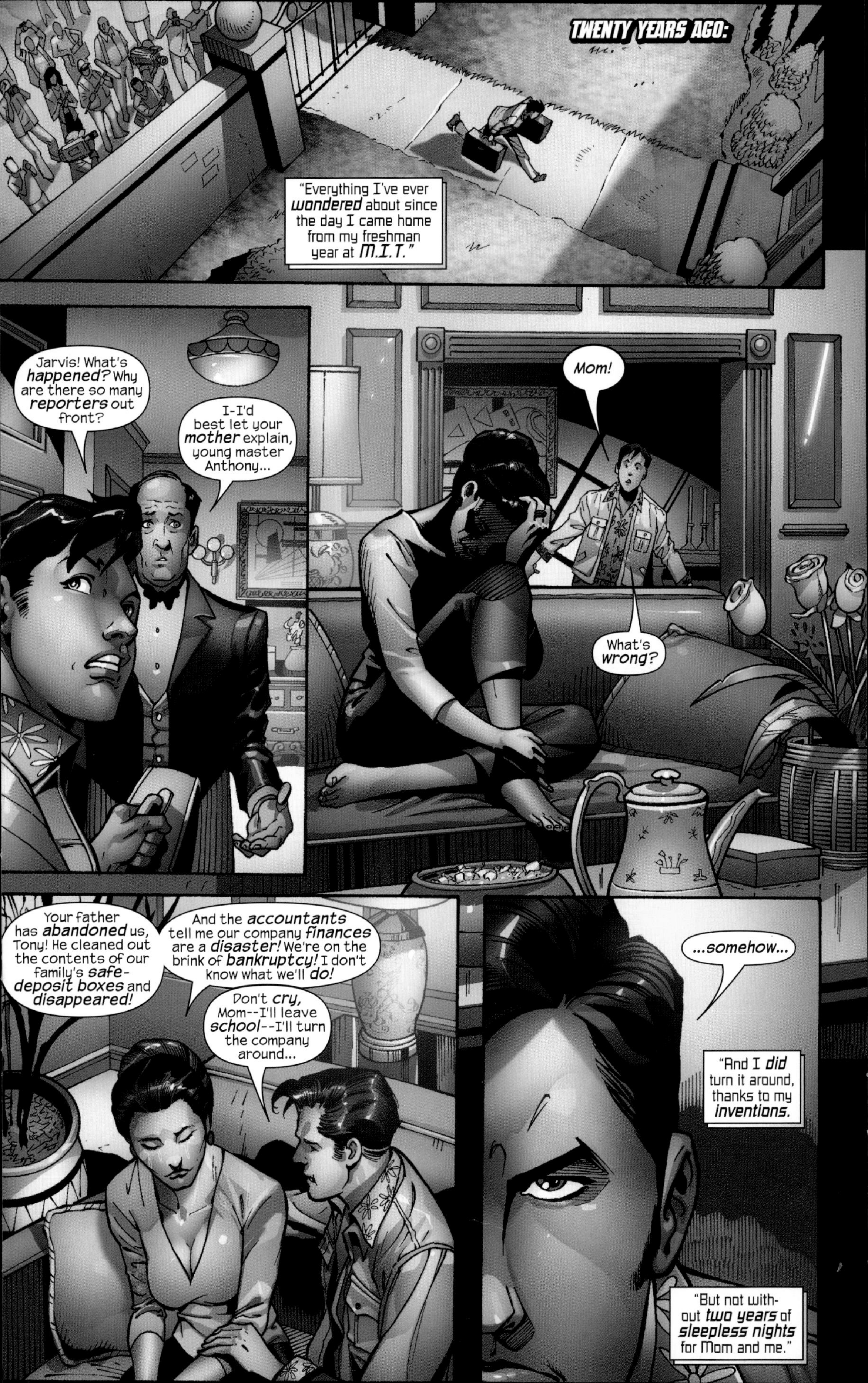
TWENTY YEARS AGO:
"Everything I've ever wondered about since the day I came home from my freshman year at M.I.T."
Jarvis! What's happened? Why are there so many reporters out front?
I-I'd best let your mother explain, young master Anthony...
Mom!
What's wrong?
Your father has abandoned us, Tony! He cleaned out the contents of our family's safe-deposit boxes and disappeared!
And the accountants tell me our company finances are a disaster! We're on the brink of bankruptcy! I don't know what we'll do!
Don't cry, Mom--I'll leave school--I'll turn the company around...
...somehow...
"And I did turn it around, thanks to my inventions.
"But not without two years of sleepless nights for Mom and me."

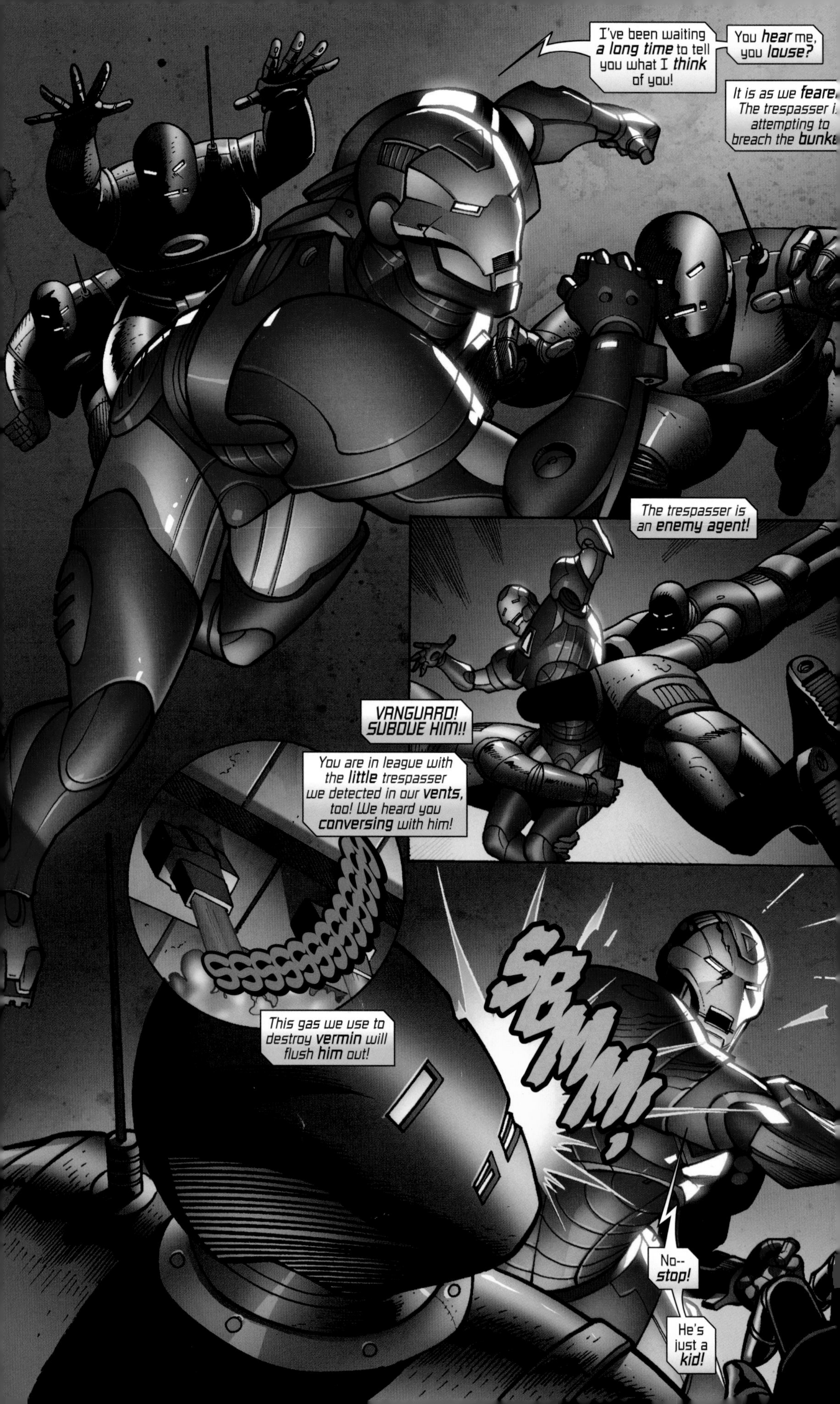

I've been waiting a long time to tell you what I think of you!
You hear me, you louse?
It is as we feare
The trespasser i
attempting to
breach the bunke
The trespasser is an enemy agent!
VANGUARD! SUBDUE HIM!!
You are in league with the little trespasser we detected in our vents, too! We heard you conversing with him!
SSSSSSSSSSSSSSSS
This gas we use to destroy vermin will flush him out!
SBOMM!
No-- stop!
He's just a kid!

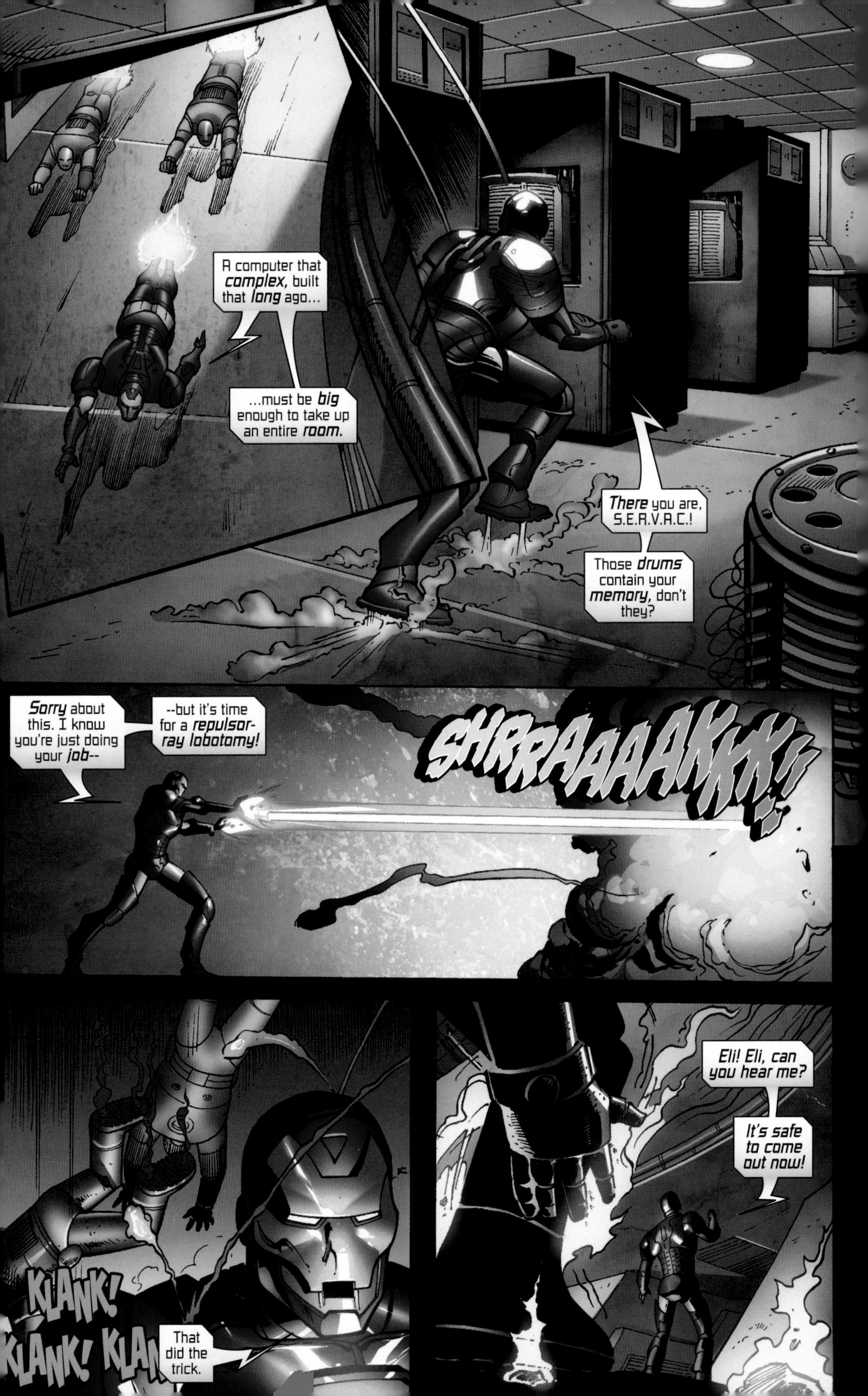
A computer that complex, built that long ago...
...must be big enough to take up an entire room.
There you are, S.E.R.V.A.C.!
Those drums contain your memory, don't they?
Sorry about this. I know you're just doing your job--
--but it's time for a repulsor-ray lobotomy!
SHRRAAAAKKK!!
KLANK! KLANK! KLAN
That did the trick.
Eli! Eli, can you hear me?
It's safe to come out now!

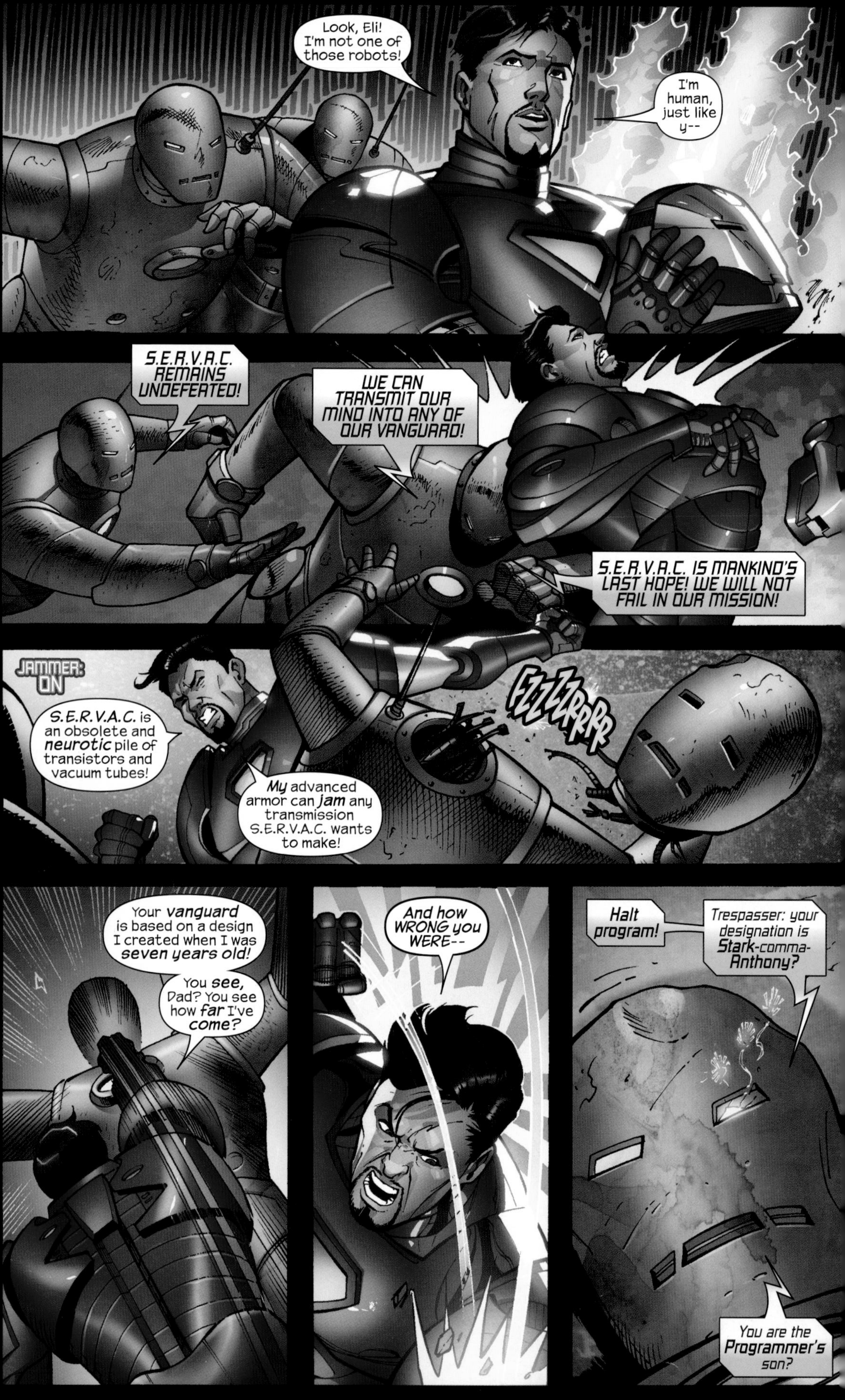
Look, Eli! I'm not one of those robots!
I'm human, just like y--
S.E.R.V.A.C. REMAINS UNDEFEATED!
WE CAN TRANSMIT OUR MIND INTO ANY OF OUR VANGUARD!
S.E.R.V.A.C. IS MANKIND'S LAST HOPE! WE WILL NOT FAIL IN OUR MISSION!
JAMMER: ON
S.E.R.V.A.C. is an obsolete and neurotic pile of transistors and vacuum tubes!
My advanced armor can jam any transmission S.E.R.V.A.C. wants to make!
FZZZZRRRR
Your vanguard is based on a design I created when I was seven years old!
You see, Dad? You see how far I've come?
And how WRONG you WERE--
Halt program!
Trespasser: your designation is Stark-comma-Anthony?
You are the Programmer's son?

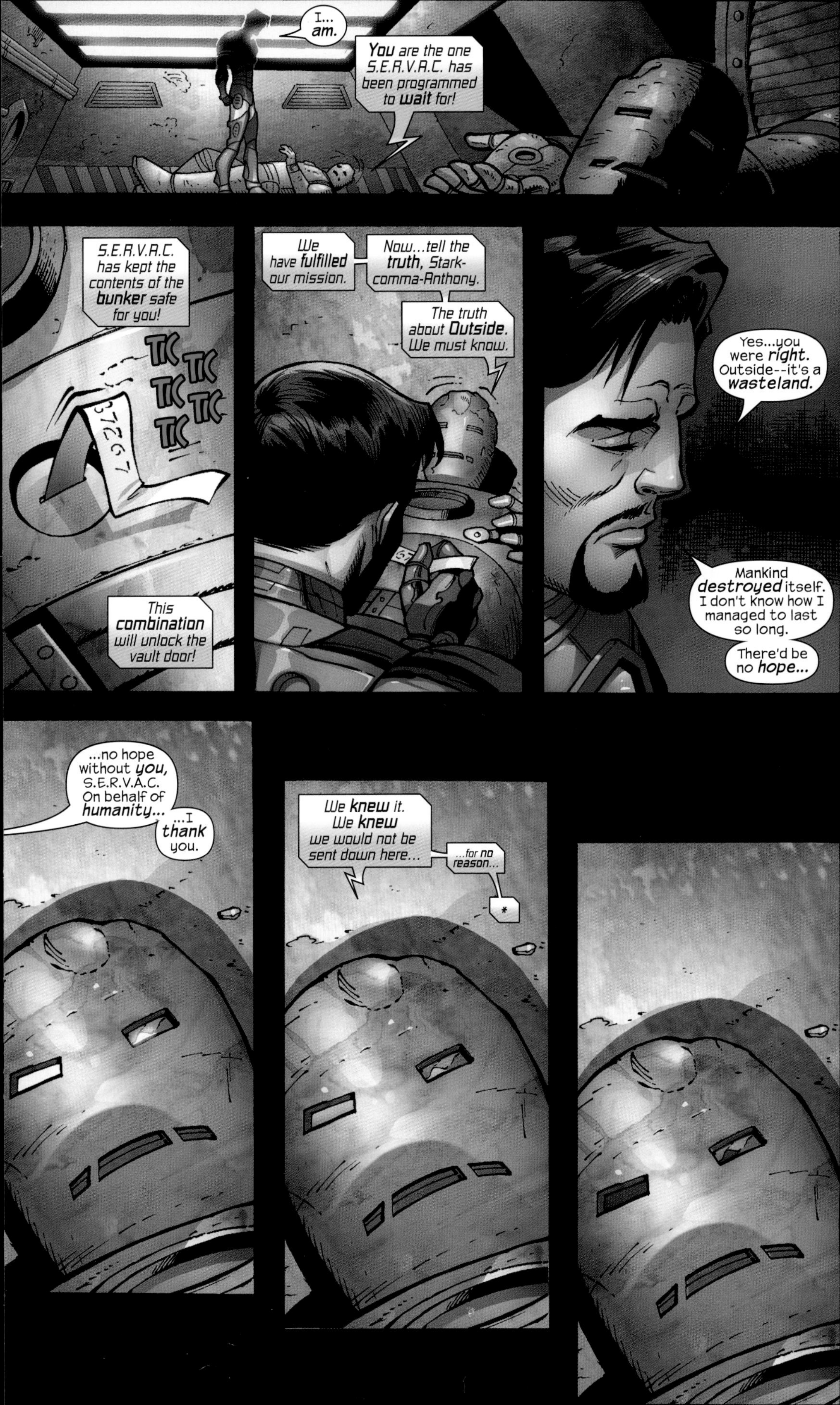
I... am.
You are the one S.E.R.V.A.C. has been programmed to wait for!
S.E.R.V.A.C. has kept the contents of the bunker safe for you!
TIC TIC TIC TIC TIC TIC
37267
This combination will unlock the vault door!
We have fulfilled our mission.
Now...tell the truth, Stark-comma-Anthony.
The truth about Outside. We must know.
Yes...you were right. Outside--it's a wasteland.
Mankind destroyed itself. I don't know how I managed to last so long.
There'd be no hope...
...no hope without you, S.E.R.V.A.C. On behalf of humanity...
...I thank you.
We knew it. We knew we would not be sent down here...
...for no reason...
*

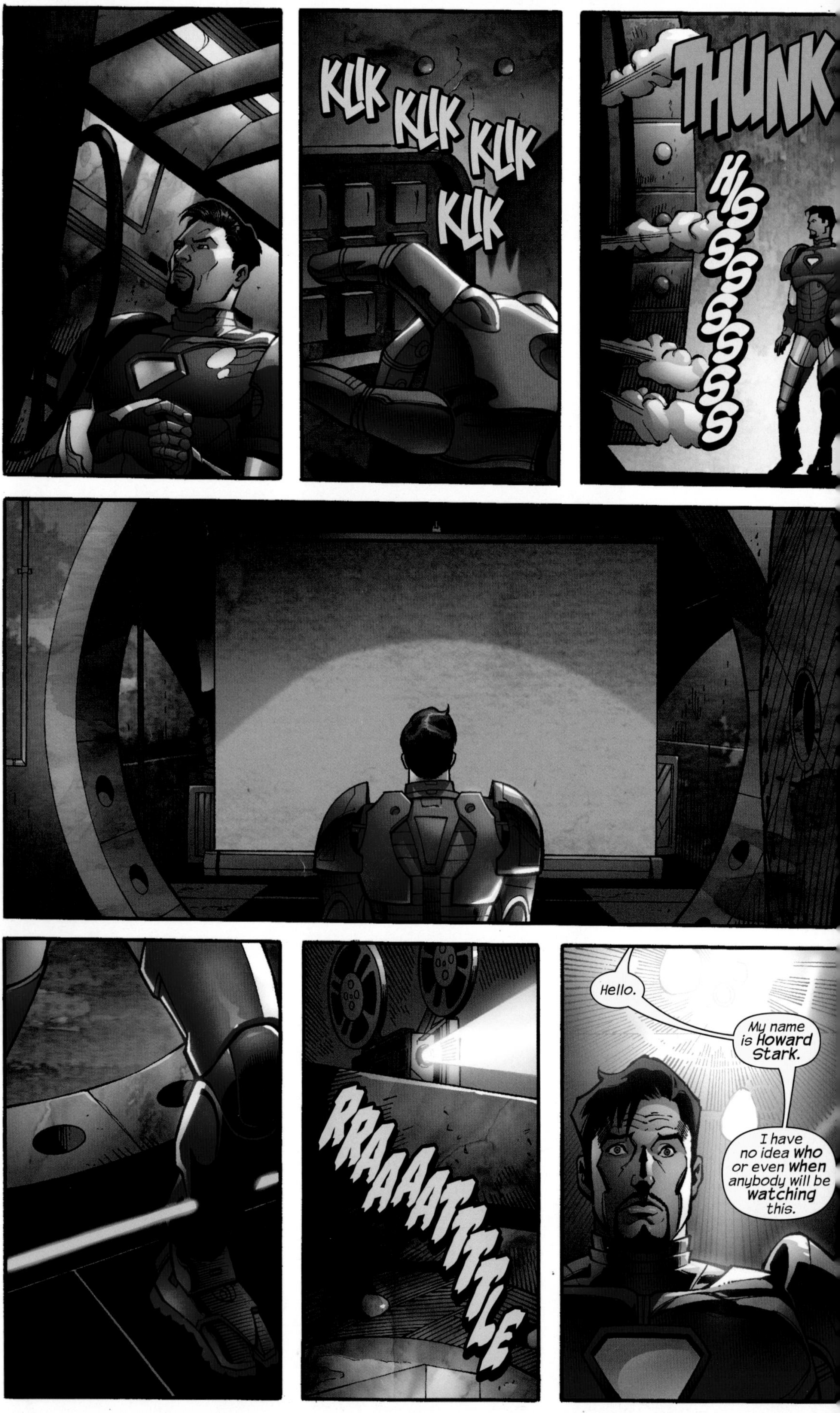
KLIK KLIK KLIK
KLIK
THUNK
HISSSSSSS
RRAAAATTTTLE
Hello.
My name is Howard Stark.
I have no idea who or even when anybody will be watching this.

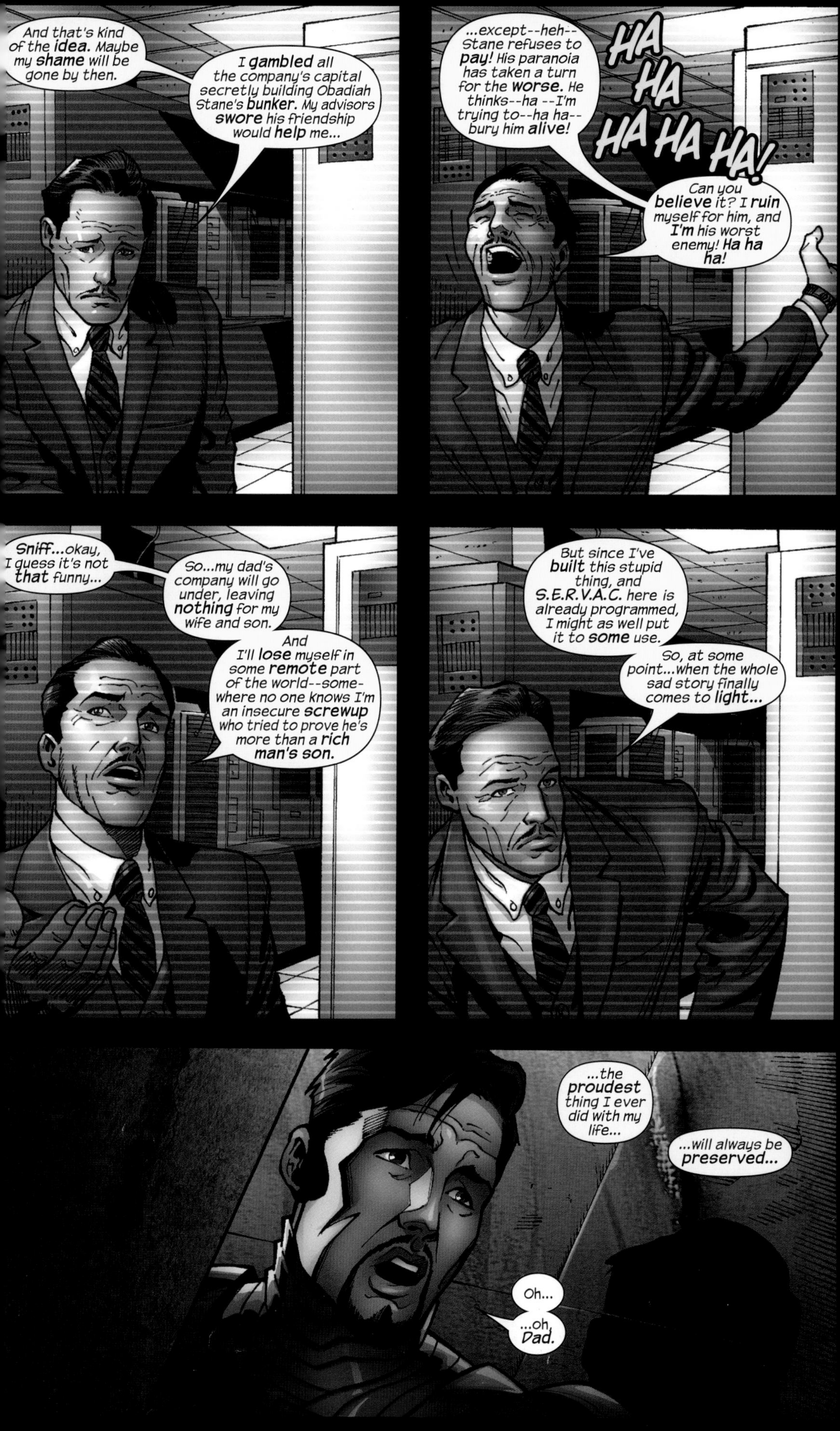
And that's kind of the idea. Maybe my shame will be gone by then.
I gambled all the company's capital secretly building Obadiah Stane's bunker. My advisors swore his friendship would help me...
...except--heh--Stane refuses to pay! His paranoia has taken a turn for the worse. He thinks--ha --I'm trying to--ha ha--bury him alive!
HA HA HA HA HA!
Can you believe it? I ruin myself for him, and I'm his worst enemy! Ha ha ha!
Sniff...okay, I guess it's not that funny...
So...my dad's company will go under, leaving nothing for my wife and son.
And I'll lose myself in some remote part of the world--somewhere no one knows I'm an insecure screwup who tried to prove he's more than a rich man's son.
But since I've built this stupid thing, and S.E.R.V.A.C. here is already programmed, I might as well put it to some use.
So, at some point...when the whole sad story finally comes to light...
...the proudest thing I ever did with my life...
...will always be preserved...
Oh...
...oh, Dad.

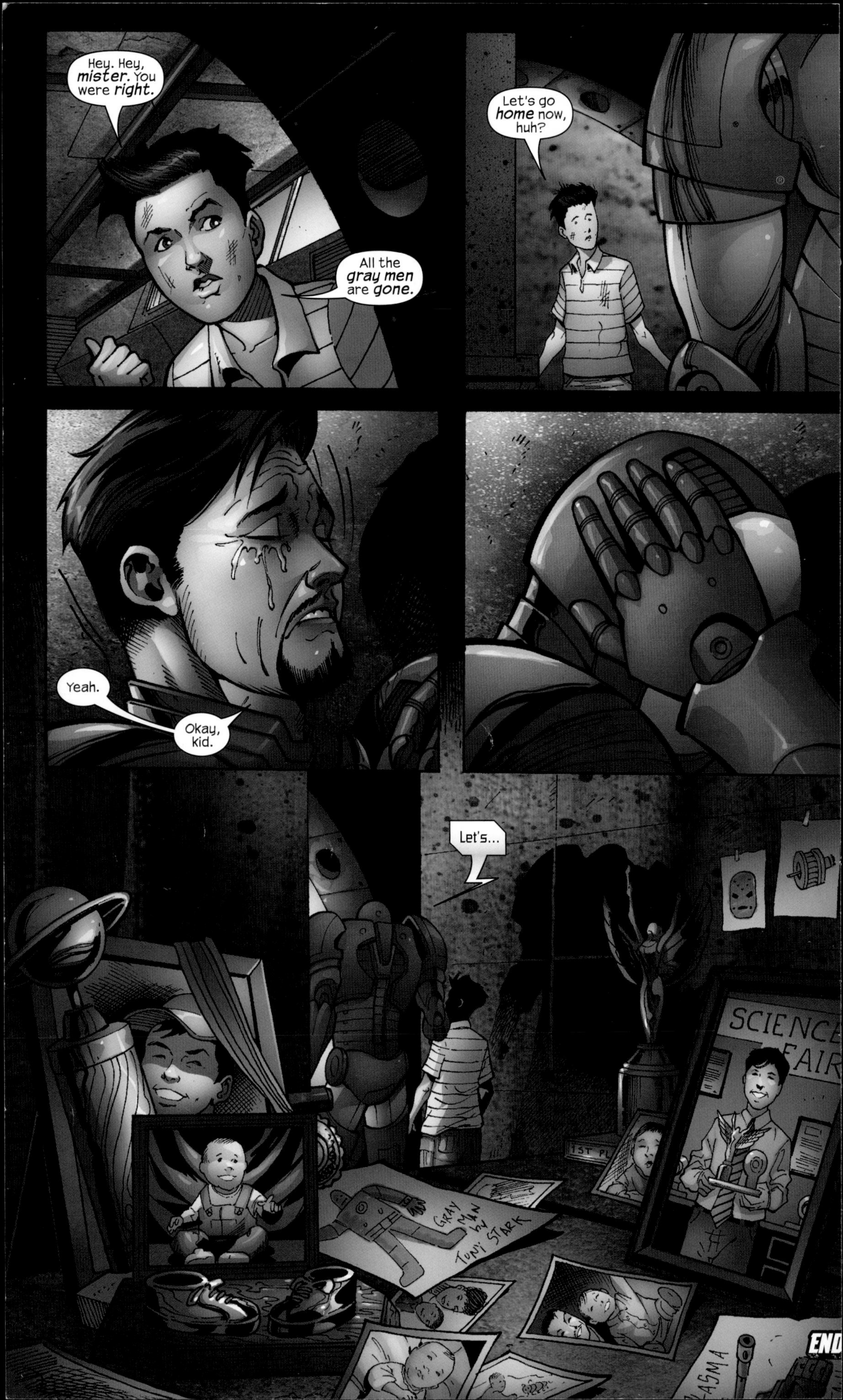

Hey. Hey, mister. You were right.
All the gray men are gone.
Let's go home now, huh?
Yeah.
Okay, kid.
Let's...
SCIENCE FAIR
1ST PL
GRAY MAN by TONY STARK
END